Dear Parent:

Congratulations! Your child is taking the first steps on an exciting journey. The destination? Independent reading!

STEP INTO READING® will help your child get there. The program offers five steps to reading success. Each step includes fun stories and colorful art. There are also Step into Reading Sticker Books, Step into Reading Math Readers, Step into Reading Phonics Readers, Step into Reading Write-In Readers, and Step into Reading Phonics Boxed Sets—a complete literacy program with something for every child.

Learning to Read, Step by Step!

Ready to Read   Preschool–Kindergarten
• big type and easy words • rhyme and rhythm • picture clues
For children who know the alphabet and are eager to begin reading.

Reading with Help   Preschool–Grade 1
• basic vocabulary • short sentences • simple stories
For children who recognize familiar words and sound out new words with help.

Reading on Your Own   Grades 1–3
• engaging characters • easy-to-follow plots • popular topics
For children who are ready to read on their own.

Reading Paragraphs   Grades 2–3
• challenging vocabulary • short paragraphs • exciting stories
For newly independent readers who read simple sentences with confidence.

Ready for Chapters   Grades 2–4
• chapters • longer paragraphs • full-color art
For children who want to take the plunge into chapter books but still like colorful pictures.

STEP INTO READING® is designed to give every child a successful reading experience. The grade levels are only guides. Children can progress through the steps at their own speed, developing confidence in their reading, no matter what their grade.

Remember, a lifetime love of reading starts with a single step!

Step into Reading, Random House, and the Random House colophon are registered trademarks
of Random House, Inc.

Visit us on the Web!
StepIntoReading.com
randomhouse.com/kids

Educators and librarians, for a variety of teaching tools, visit us at RHTeachersLibrarians.com

ISBN 978-0-7364-8128-1 (trade) — ISBN 978-0-7364-2984-9 (lib. bdg.)
Printed in the United States of America   10 9 8 7 6 5 4 3 2 1

DISNEP
PRINCESS

THE LITTLE MERMAID

By Ruth Homberg

Illustrated by the Disney Storybook Artists

Random House 🏠 New York

Ariel is a mermaid.

She is also a princess.

Flounder is her friend.

Scuttle is her friend, too.
He teaches Ariel
about humans.

Ariel dreams of life
above the sea.

King Triton
is Ariel's father.
He is angry
with Ariel.

He does not
trust humans.
He wants Ariel
to stay home.

At night,
Ariel swims
above the water.
There is a storm.

She sees a human.

His name is Prince Eric.

He falls off a ship!

Ariel saves Eric.

Ariel sings
to Eric.
She falls in love
with him.

Ursula is an evil witch.

She takes Ariel's voice.

She gives Ariel legs.

Ariel must kiss Eric.

She has three days.

If they do not kiss,

she will lose her legs

and her voice forever.

Ariel is human!

She can live on land.

She loves her new legs.

Ariel's friends help her.
Scuttle makes
her a dress.

Eric is looking
for the girl
who sang to him.
He thinks it is Ariel.
But she has no voice.

Eric brings Ariel
to the palace.

She combs her hair
with a fork!
Eric laughs.
He likes Ariel.

Eric and Ariel
go on a boat ride.
They almost kiss.

Ursula's eels tip
the boat over!

Ursula does not want
Eric to kiss Ariel.
She changes herself.
She uses Ariel's voice.

Eric loves her voice.
He thinks he is in love
with Ursula!

Eric is going
to marry Ursula!
Scuttle finds out
about her trick.

Scuttle and his friends
stop Ursula.

Ariel's voice is back!

It is too late.

She turns

into a mermaid again.

Ursula laughs.

She turns
into a huge monster!
Eric stops her for good.

King Triton wants Ariel
to be happy.

He makes her
human again.

Eric loves Ariel.
Now they can be
together forever.

Eric and Ariel live
happily ever after!